Usborne
Greek
Myths
for Little
Children

Usborne
Greek
Myths
for Little
Children

Retold by **Rosie Dickins**

Illustrated by **Sara Ugolotti**

Contents

Pandora's Box

Do NOT open this box!

In the beginning, the gods
lived above the clouds on
Mount Olympus and people
lived below on Earth.

A giant called Prometheus felt sorry
for the people. He watched them shiver
through cold meals and colder nights.

Then he went to his brother,
Epimetheus, and they hatched a plan.

Prometheus crept up
to Mount Olympus
and stole a spark from
the gods' own fire.

Quickly and quietly,
he carried his burning
stick back to Earth.

The people were thrilled.

"Now we can keep warm and cook. We'll live like gods!"

But Zeus, king
of the gods,
was FURIOUS.

"I'll show them what happens when someone steals from ME!"

He sent a magical eagle to snatch up
Prometheus, and chained him
to a mountainside.

Zeus had a different punishment
for Epimetheus.

On the giant's wedding day,
Zeus sent the bride a gift...

It was a decorated
wooden box. And it came
with a warning.

The bride's name was Pandora.
She was pretty and clever, and
she loved to find things out.

The more she thought
about the box, the more
she LONGED to open it.

"WHY give someone a box
if they can't open it?"

"There may be NOTHING in it," she thought. "But if that's true why shouldn't I look?"

"And what if it contains something IMPORTANT? Then I should DEFINITELY look."

In the end, Pandora could not resist. She lifted the lid...

"Oh no!"

WHOC

OOSH!

Dark, shadowy
shapes billowed out.

Angry Zeus had
filled the box with
troubles and torments,
KNOWING Pandora
would open it.

Now the troubles had escaped into the world. People's lives would never be carefree again.

Pandora slammed the lid and
gazed at the box in horror.

Then she heard a noise.

Something was
fluttering inside.

Whatever it was, it didn't
sound big or dangerous.

Taking a deep breath,
Pandora raised the
lid again...

Out flew a tiny
winged creature.

It glowed with a warm
light, making her heart lift.

The creature was Hope – and Pandora's
quick-thinking had kept it safe.

So, despite their new troubles, the people
of Earth would always have hope.

King Midas
and the Gold

King Midas loved three
things above all else.

His gold...

his roses...

...and his little
daughter, Zoe.

One day, Midas and Zoe
were walking among
the roses when
they heard
a rumble...

Zzzzz

Zoe ran to see what
it was – and almost
tripped over a
pair of dusty feet.

There was an old man with
rumpled hair and crumpled robes.

Yawn...

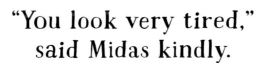

"You look very tired,"
said Midas kindly.

"Why don't you come
and stay with us?
You can have a
meal and sleep in
a proper bed."

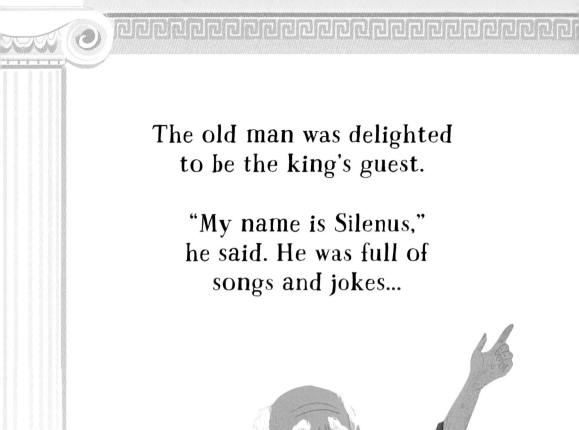

The old man was delighted
to be the king's guest.

"My name is Silenus,"
he said. He was full of
songs and jokes...

"A man wanted to see
how he looked asleep.
So, he looked in the mirror
with his eyes CLOSED!"

"Ha ha!"

Silenus stayed at the palace for three nights. On the fourth day...

"Silenus!"

"Dionysus!"

...someone came looking for him.

It was his friend, Dionysus.

Midas gazed in awe. Dionysus was a GOD.

"What happened to you?"
asked Dionysus.

"I got lost," admitted
Silenus. "But Midas here
took good care of me."

The god thanked the king.

"In return, I grant you a wish. **Anything!** What shall it be?"

Midas didn't hesitate.
"I wish for whatever I touch
to turn into GOLD."

Dionysus raised an eyebrow.
"Are you SURE?"

Midas nodded.

"Very well."

"What shall I try first?"
wondered Midas.
His eye fell on a rose...

One touch, and its soft petals
hardened to a golden shine.

Midas danced around,
whooping, until the whole
garden gleamed with gold.

He saw a tree
covered in apples.

"Those look tasty"
he thought,
picking one...

"Ow!"

He was biting
a lump of cold,
hard gold.

Thirsty, he tried to
take a drink...

"Oh no..."

The water turned to gold
before it touched his lips.

Now Zoe was running towards
him, arms outstretched...

"STOP!" he cried.

Too late – his little daughter
was a golden statue.

Midas stared in horror.
Then he ran to find Dionysus.

"Please, I beg you,
take back your gift."

The god nodded.

"Wash your hands in the river," he said, "and the gift will wash away."

Midas raced to
the riverbank
and plunged in
his hands.

A swirl of gold
appeared in the water.

At the same time,
the gold in his garden faded.

Zoe blinked and smiled as Midas
swept her up in a huge hug,

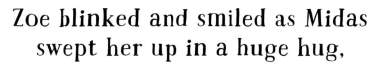

"Zoe!

I have learned my lesson.
YOU are more precious
than any gold."

The First Olive Tree

Hammering and shouts filled the air.

Slowly but
surely, strong
walls and
graceful
columns were
appearing.

A new city was being built,
and it looked SPLENDID.

The gods looked down
eagerly from above.

They knew that soon
the people would
need a god for
the new city.

The people would build
this god a special temple
and fill it with gifts.

In return, they hoped
the god would watch over
and protect their city.

But the gods couldn't agree
WHO should be chosen.

"They are building by the sea,"
roared Poseidon, god of the sea.

"They should
worship ME!"

"They are clever," argued
Athena, goddess of wisdom.

"They should
choose ME!"

Poseidon raised
his trident.

"I'll fight you for it!"

Athena shook her head.
"I have a better idea. Let the
people choose! We will each
give the city a present.

Whoever gives the
best present will be
the city's god."

Poseidon pictured the
wonderful things
he could give.

"Endless fish?"

"Fair winds for
their ships?"

"A new kind
of animal?"

"I know... WATER!
Humans can't live
without it."

"All right,"

he told Athena.
"The best present wins!"

Athena thought hard
about her present.
She knew the people
of the city would
need many things.

"Food to eat,
wood to make things
and to burn on their fires,
oil to light their lamps..."

"Perhaps I can give them ALL of those?"

The next day, the rivals
appeared before the people.
Poseidon spoke first.

"People of the city,
I bring you a gift!"

He hurled his trident
at a rocky crag.

crRRRRACK!

The rock shattered,
and a stream of clear,
cold water spurted out.

People hurried over to try
the water – then spluttered
and spat it out again.

Poseidon, god of the
sea, had given the
city SEA water.

"Ugh!"

"It's salty."

"Thank you, but...
we can't drink this."

Poseidon scowled.
"How ungrateful!" he huffed.
"On second thoughts, I DON'T
want to be god of these people."

Then Athena spoke.
"I too come
with a gift."

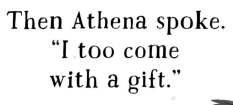

She pointed
at the ground.
A shoot burst out.

Quickly
it twisted
higher,

sprouting

branches,

silvery leaves

and **dark** berries.

"I give you the first OLIVE tree."

"Its fruit will feed you.
Crush the fruit, and it
will make golden oil.

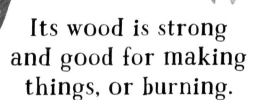

Its wood is strong
and good for making
things, or burning.

And its silver leaves
will dance in the wind,
to gladden your hearts."

The people were delighted.

"Hurray!"

"THANK YOU!"

"Athena, **you** are our goddess!
We will name our city
Athens after you."

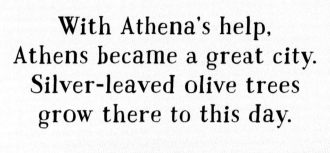

With Athena's help,
Athens became a great city.
Silver-leaved olive trees
grow there to this day.

Arion and the Dolphin

Arion was no ordinary musician.
When he played, EVERYONE
stopped to listen.

He could charm the birds out of
the trees and the wild animals
from the forest.

The king loved Arion's music most of all.

"Aaah, beautiful..."

One day, Arion announced
he was leaving for a
distant island.

"NO! Why?"
spluttered the king.

"There's a competition,"
Arion explained.
"To find the best musician."

"Promise you will
come back?"

Arion nodded.
"I promise."

Arion went down to the shore
to find a ship and sailors.

Seabirds swooped and waves
swooshed as they set sail.

When they arrived, the island was abuzz with all kinds of musicians.

Some were **very** good.

Some were **terrible!**

Then Arion stepped onto the stage.
His soft, sweet tunes rippled
through the air, enchanting
all who listened.

When he finished,
the winner
was clear.

"ARION!"

"ARION!"

Arion returned to his ship with
the winner's crown and a bag of gold.

The sailors eyed the gold greedily.
Out at sea, they began to plot.

"Let's grab that bag and
throw HIM overboard!"

Arion tried to delay them.

"Let me play
one last tune,"
he begged.

Curious to hear
the famous musician,
the sailors agreed.

Arion began a sad, beautiful tune.
Its haunting notes made the sailors shiver.

Overhead, the
seabirds joined in
with mournful cries.

In the foaming waters around the ship,
sleek blue dolphins gathered to listen.

As the final notes died away,
the sailors moved in.

Arion dodged and
sprang over the side...

SPLOSH!

Arion splashed and spluttered.

The sailors laughed as they sailed
away. "He'll never catch us now.
The **gold** is ours!"

Moments later, a great blue
dolphin rose up beneath Arion,
lifting him out of the water.

He clung to its fin as it sped
swiftly towards the shore.

In the safety of the shallows,
Arion sprang down.
The dolphin had
saved his life!

"Goodbye, my friend,
and thank you!"

The king was delighted
to see Arion again.

"Tell me **ALL** about your
trip," he begged.

So Arion did.

When the king heard
about the sailors, he
turned to his guards.

"Bring those scoundrels
here," he ordered.
"Don't let them know
Arion is alive.
I have a plan..."

The king greeted
the sailors sternly.

"Where is Arion?"

"He's not coming
home," they lied.
"He's, um... having
too much fun."

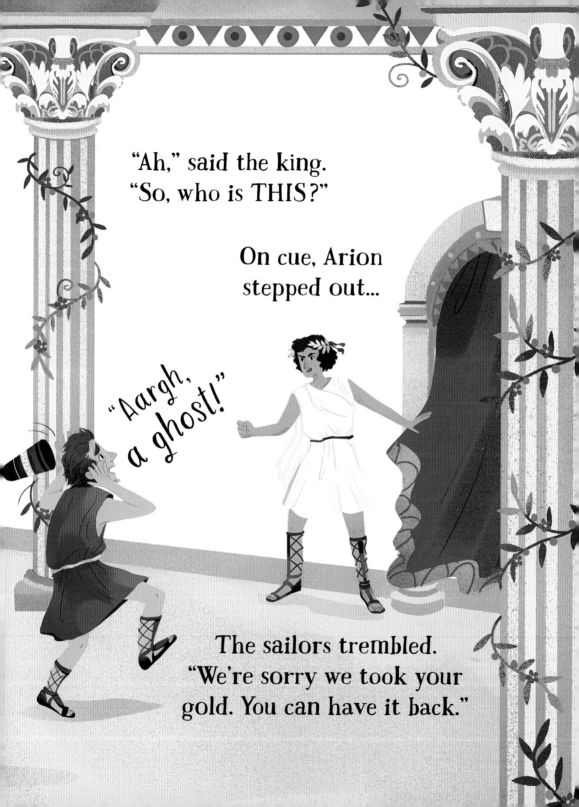

"You will return EVERYTHING you stole," ordered the king. "Then you will leave my kingdom FOREVER!"

So Arion got back his prize and lived happily ever after.

Often, on warm evenings, he would
go down to the shore and play...

...and a great **blue dolphin**
would leap up from the
waves and dance.

Heracles
and the VERY Smelly Stables

The King of Elis was proud of
his son, Prince Phyleus. But he was
even more proud of his cattle.

He owned THOUSANDS –
beautiful, big beasts, with
gleaming golden coats.

They spent their days
grazing the lush river meadows
around his palace...

...and their nights
in his enormous
stone stables.

There was just one problem.
The stables had NEVER been cleaned.

At first, the king's servants
had put it off.

"We'll do it tomorrow."

As the dung piled higher,
they became afraid to try.

"We can't clean
THAT!"

"It's too big
a job!"

But the cattle
had to spend the
night somewhere...
so the dung heaps
kept growing.

As years passed,
the stables became
ever more filthy.
Swarms of flies buzzed
around MOUNTAINS of dung.

As for the smell...

"EUURGH!"

The king
just shrugged.

THAT was when Heracles arrived.

Heracles was the STRONGEST man
in Greece. He could wrestle lions and
conquer monsters. And for his next task...

The king scowled.
He was a tight-fisted tyrant,
and hated paying
for anything.

"But the stables
DO smell awful...

and surely NO ONE
can clean them in
a day – not even
Heracles!"

At last, the king nodded.
"Very well. A hundred cattle IF
you finish by sunset. My son will
go with you, to see there's
no cheating!"

Heracles bowed, concealing a grin.
He hadn't become a hero simply by
being strong. He was cunning, too.
And he had a plan...

"Come on, Phyleus."

To find the stables, Heracles just had to follow his nose.

"UGH!"

He went up to the stable wall and raised his club...

SMASH! CRASH!

Stones crumbled to smithereens, leaving a ragged hole.

He climbed through it to reach the wall opposite.

BASH! SMASH!

Another hole.

Heracles dropped the club
and grabbed a shovel.
Then, he began to dig.

Clods of dirt and
clumps of grass flew
through the air.

Heracles dug all the way
across the meadows
to the river.

Long before sunset, he was ready. He dug
out the last remaining chunks of soil...

River water gushed into the channel, swirling and speeding towards the stables.

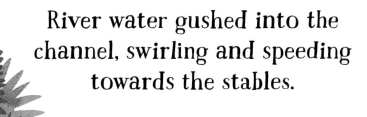

SWOOOOSH!

It rushed through the hole in the wall, sweeping up everything inside – straw, dirt, dung...

A moment later, it ALL
fountained out of the
hole opposite.

WHOOOOSH!

Phyleus gasped as
the mountains of dung
simply washed away.

Once everything was sparkling,
Heracles filled in the holes in the walls.

Then, he went to collect
his payment.

"I'm NOT handing over
my royal cattle to a
DUNG sweeper,"
snapped the king.

"Get out of here before
I have you locked up!"

"But Dad, you PROMISED!"

Heracles smiled
at the prince.

"This boy will make
a fine king some day."

Heracles left, only to return at
the head of a powerful army.

"This land needs a better ruler —
and I'm here to see it gets one!"

When he saw the army, the old king fled...

"Long live King Phyleus!"

Phyleus and Heracles remained firm friends. And the stables? Phyleus made sure they never got so dirty again.

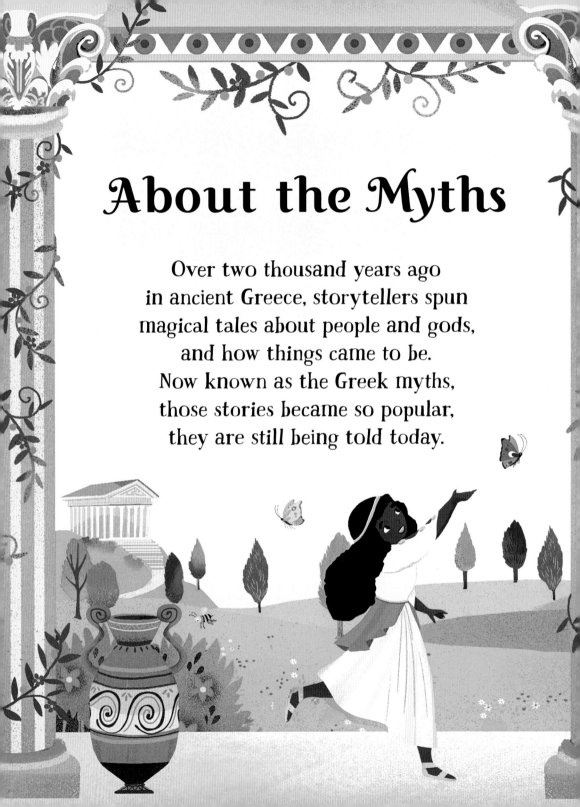

About the Myths

Over two thousand years ago
in ancient Greece, storytellers spun
magical tales about people and gods,
and how things came to be.
Now known as the Greek myths,
those stories became so popular,
they are still being told today.

Usborne Quicklinks

Ancient Greek names can be tricky to say.
To hear any of the names from this book,
or to find out more about ancient Greece,
go to: usborne.com/Quicklinks
and type in the title of this book.

Please follow the internet safety
guidelines at Usborne Quicklinks.
Children should be supervised online.

Designed by Lenka Hrehova & Tabitha Blore
Digital imaging: Nick Wakeford
Series designer: Russell Punter
Series editor: Lesley Sims

First published in 2022 by Usborne Publishing Ltd.,
83-85 Saffron Hill, London EClN 8RT, England. usborne.com
Copyright © 2022 Usborne Publishing Ltd. The name Usborne
and the Balloon logo are Trade Marks of Usborne Publishing Ltd.
All rights reserved. No part of this publication may be reproduced,
stored in a retrieval system, or transmitted in any form or by
any means, without the prior permission of the publisher. UE.

Usborne Publishing is not responsible for the availability or content
of any website other than its own, or for any exposure to harmful,
offensive or inaccurate material which may appear on the Web.